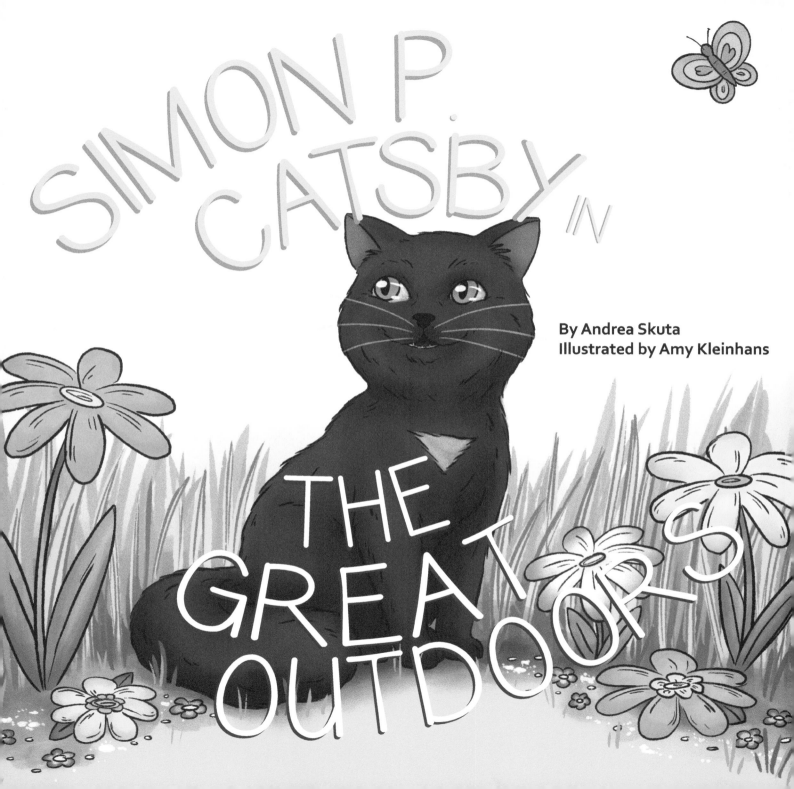

SIMON P. CATSBY in

THE GREAT OUTDOORS

By Andrea Skuta

Illustrated by Amy Kleinhans

Published by Orange Hat Publishing 2022
ISBN 9781645384083

www.orangehatpublishing.com

DEDICATION
In memory of my Grandma Diana, who taught me
a love of reading, writing, and everything outdoors.
I am forever grateful for these gifts from you.

Simon silently stared out his favorite window. Deer grazed, bunnies played, and birds chirped in his backyard. He loved watching the outdoors from inside his safe home. Simon waited for his family to return from their daily walk.

He remembered the outside as cold, loud, and lonely. He was too scared to venture back out there. No matter how many times Ms. Catsby tried, Simon refused.

"Simon Patrick Catsby, let's GO!"

Simon's life indoors was as purrfect as could be.

...or so he thought.

At dinnertime, Simon overheard his family excitedly talking about the new boys coming soon. The conversation seemed strange to him. And, where was Ms. Catsby?

His radar ears heard jangling keys
and the squeaking doorknob.

Two small puppies burst through the front door and
hopped, bounced, then ran straight to Simon.

"Simon, meet your two new brothers, Axl and Slash."

Simon scrambled under the sofa, screeching and hissing as the puppies chased him. Mad and scared, Simon wondered why he deserved such a CATastrophe.

Two days later, his rumbling, empty stomach forced him out of hiding. The house was quiet, and Simon hoped he was finally alone.

After nearly emptying his food bowl, Simon crept to his favorite window again, the best place to be.

Just as he drifted into a nice cat nap, a loud BANG startled him, and Simon tumbled to the floor!

Axl and Slash had returned from the family walk outside, back to terrorize him.

Day after day, Simon experienced new frustrations.

His brothers stole
his hair ties,

But those are my
favorite toys!

WOOF! Grrrr!

barked way too loudly,

and left doggy drool
in his water bowl.

Simon needed some time alone. Desperately.

Simon slowly sulked to the doorway. He secretly slid open the screen door. He poked his nose out, flexed his whiskers, and sniffed.

First one paw, then the other.
Before he could step outside,
Simon felt his heart thumping.

His fear took over. Simon scurried
back under the blankets—sad,
scared, and defeated.

As time went on, Simon's frustrations with his brothers slowly faded. He learned Axl and Slash were quite warm and snuggly. His NEW favorite toy was their wagging tails. And he always won the game of Hide and Seek.

When the family walked each day, Simon found himself growing sad. It looked like fun exploring the outdoors together, but he still couldn't make his scaredy-cat self go outside.

From his favorite window, the sound of laughter made his sensitive ears t-w-i-t-c-h.

Slowly opening one bright green eye, Simon saw Axl and Slash running silly and free, weaving in and out of his family as they played in his backyard.

For the first time in his kitty life, Simon wished he was brave enough to join them.

Then a funny thing happened. One evening, as Simon chased his brothers in a heated game of tag, Ms. Catsby opened the door for the family to go on their walk.

Halfway across his beloved backyard, Simon froze in terror. Axl and Slash ran back to him.

They nuzzled Simon and wagged their tails. Simon felt calmer and safe. He looked around and listened.

He saw the deer grazing and bunnies playing.

He heard the birds chirping.

And…he was outside with them.

Joined by Axl, Slash, and his family trailing behind,
Simon bravely went on his first family walk outside.

He realized how purrfect his life now was with his new brothers and his newfound courage. Turns out, all he needed was help from two silly dogs!

He may have even met a new
friend in the great outdoors…